Vacation Adventure Girl #1

Adventure Hilton Head

The Legend of the Dolphin Locket

* * *

by Ginger Fox

Interior Illustrations by
Jules Turknett

STORY-GO-ROUND PUBLISHING / ATLANTA

Story-Go-Round Publishing
Atlanta, GA

www.vacationadventuregirl.com

Publisher's Note: This is a work of fiction. Names, characters, places, and incidents are a product of the author's imagination. Locales and public names are sometimes used for atmospheric purposes. Any resemblance to actual people, living or dead, or to businesses, companies, events, institutions, or locales is completely coincidental.

Ordering Information: Special discounts are available on quantity purchases by corporations, associations, and others. For details, contact the publisher at the above website.

Atlanta / Ginger Fox — First Edition

ISBN: 1512241555

Printed in the United States of America

For Jules and Tucker,
Our own Maddie and Mikey

Become a
Vacation Adventure Girl

Be the first to know where the next vacation adventure takes place! Head over to vacationadventuregirl.com/club to find out. There you can also sign up for the Vacation Adventure Girls Club to receive the latest Vacation Adventure Girl news, get special bonuses just for club members, and receive an early copy of the next book in the series.

Summer Surprise

I can't believe it's finally here! Well, it'll be here in five minutes, that is. Five very loooonnng minutes.

I'm talking, of course, about summer break! Five more minutes, well four now, and school is out for the summer. For me, that means the end of third grade!

It's not that I didn't like third grade, though I don't like the waking up early every day part. Nor do I like it when Danny Davis chases me on the playground and tells me he loves me. "Will you marry me, Maddie?!!" Ugh.

But I do like school. Especially library time. I love, love, love, LOVE books. Okay, so don't tell anybody this (like my mom!), but sometimes I wake up in the middle of the night and instead of going back to sleep, I turn on my book light and read. Sometimes for hours. And then I have to pretend I'm not tired the next day so my mom won't be suspicious!

And I love nature class, too. I love exploring in the woods and I love animals. And bugs. I know I'm a girl and I'm supposed to be scared of things like worms and spiders, but I'm not. Not one bit. I like to hold them in my hand all wiggling around and freak out the scaredy-cat boys.

Speaking of animals, I have two cats, Butterpaws and Fluffles. And I have a Furby named Minloo, but I suppose she doesn't count as an animal. I love her just the same, though. She's such a chatterbox.

But my favorite animal? Dolphins.

Which is why I'm soooo excited about school being out, because we're going to my favorite vacation place in the world. A place where I always get to see LOTS of dolphins. It's called Hilton Head Island.

I've been going there with my family every summer since I was born, and now we always go as soon as school gets out. That means we'll pack up tonight and head out first thing tomorrow!

Actually, I'm already packed. I finished two days ago and I've had my suitcases sitting by the front door ever since. I know this kind of drives my mom crazy, but I can't help it. I'm so excited!

Brrrriinng. Oh, there it is! The school bell. It's official now, summer is here!

"Bye, Ms. Applebottom," I say, "I'll see you next year!" I'm trying my best not to run, but I'm ready to sprint out of here.

"Bye, Maddie," Ms. Applebottom replies. "Have a great summer!"

Now, usually my mom picks me up from school, so I was a little puzzled when I saw our car in the carpool line and Dad was driving. What's he doing here? Shouldn't he be at work? He doesn't usually get home for a couple more hours.

And what's that on the top of our car? Looks like our rooftop suitcase carrier. But dad never packs that until... WE'RE READY TO LEAVE FOR VACATION!

*
*   *
*

2

Are we there yet?

inally! My parents pull to the front of the line and the teachers call us to get in the car. "Us" being me and my super annoying little brother Mikey. After he climbs in, I follow and lob questions at my folks, "Why is dad here? Why is the car packed? Are we leaving today? Are we? Are we, are we, are we?" I barely pause to breathe between my questions. There's so much I need to know, like now!

My parents chuckle and tell me, "Yes, Maddie Mack. Surprise! We are heading to Hilton Head today -- right now!"

Wahoo! Here we go!

Wait! "Did you grab my phone and my earbuds? Did you remember my books? What about the pool noodles?" I have so many questions. I need to make sure that we have everything. We need everything to make our vacation perfect!

"Yes, Maddie," my parents reassure me. "We've got it all covered."

"Who's taking care of Butterpaws and Fluffles?" I HAVE to make sure that my furry little felines are well cared for. I love those two little guys. No one understands me like those two do. They just GET me. I wish they could come with us.

"Yes, Maddie," my mom sighs. "We met with the pet sitters this morning. They will come check on Butterpaws and Fluffles every day. The kitties will be just fine."

Okay, now that I know that everything is squared away, it's time to launch into full-on-excitement mode! Hilton Head! Yay! I LOVE Hilton Head! I can't wait! There's so much to do there!

I look at my little brother and we grin at each other. Sometimes Mikey and I don't get along. But right now, as members of the Gregg Russell fan club, we both know it's time to start "Operation Annoy the Parents" just like always. Hey, it's tradition.

You see, Gregg Russell is this awesome singer at Hilton Head who performs just for kids. He gives us tips to drive our parents crazy in the car -- and they work!

"Are we there yet? Are we there yet? Are we there? Are we there?" we sing at the top of our lungs. We can only manage the first line, then we start laughing so hard we can barely breathe. Our parents don't seem to be enjoying this as much as we are. But that's kind of the point.

"Blame it on Gregg Russell, Mom and Dad," I giggle. "It was his idea!"

3

A Plan

O kay, first thing's first. I need to make a plan. A plan of what, you ask? Of all the things we HAVE to do while we're in Hilton Head. Here's my list:

1. See Gregg Russell show
2. Ride horses at Lawton Stables
3. Shop at Harbour Town
4. Go swimming
5. Ride bikes to the Forest Preserve
6. Ride the Trolley
7. Tie dye a Salty Dog Shirt
8. Get ice cream
9. Avoid Mikey (mikey, if you are reading this, scram!)

And Last But Not Least...

10. SEE THE DOLPHINS !!!

4

Gator Goons

"You're laying on my arm!" Mikey screams, jolting me awake. Here I am taking a nice comfy nap, and Mikey has to ruin it. "Mikey, I didn't mean to. I was sleeping."

Didn't I tell you he's annoying?

After I settle down from my irritating-little-brother moment, I turn to look out the window. I must've been asleep for a while, because I see we're already crossing the bridge to Hilton Head Island!

"Mom and Dad, we're here, we're here!" I shout.

"We know!" they both smile, "I guess you don't need to sing 'Are We There Yet' anymore."

I can't believe we got here so fast. I wave to the guard at the gate to Sea Pines as we drive through. He gives my dad a military-style salute to let him know he can drive in, and then winks at me as we pass. Sea Pines is the place inside Hilton Head where we've stayed for the past few years. There's so much to do here.

There's the ocean, of course. But there are also bike trails everywhere, swimming pools, shopping (did I mention I LOVE to buy stuff?), a huge forest, and lots of wild animals like deer, turtles, blue herons, and...

"Gator goon!" I yell.

"What's that, Maddie?" my parents ask.

"There's an alligator over there on the edge of that lagoon," I say

"Whoa!" says Mikey. "He's huuuge!"

"So what's a 'gator goon', Maddie?" my Dad questions.

"A lagoon where an alligator lives, silly." I tease.

My parents laugh. "Did you make that up yourself, Maddie Mack?" they ask.

"I guess so," I reply. "Why?"

"That's just really clever," my Dad chuckles.

"Thanks," I say. I can feel my cheeks get red. I always feel shy when people compliment me, even if it's just my parents.

"Hey mom, what's that smell?" Mikey asks.

I smell it, too. Smells like something is burning. I've never smelled a burning smell in Hilton Head before.

"I think you're smelling the wildfires," my Mom says. "They've been having a problem here with them lately."

"Wildfires?!" I ask. That doesn't sound good at all. "What if our villa catches fire?!"

"No, sweetie," my mom says, "The fires have only been in the forests. The firefighters have been putting them out, but they keep coming back. Nobody is quite sure why."

"The poor animals," I say.

"Animals?" my dad asks.

"Yeah, the forest is their home. Without the forest, where would they live? The animals are one of my favorite things about coming here."

Finally, we pull into the parking lot of our villa. I'm super excited to be here, but I have to say, all that business about the wildfires has me a little worried.

*
*
*
*

5

Dolphin Watch

We've been staying in the same villa here for as long as I can remember. It's right next to the South Beach Marina, where they have the BEST ice cream stand! I always get cookies-and-cream and Mikey likes the bright blue Superman ice cream.

They also have lots of gift shops at the marina. And you won't believe this: one has real, live hermit crabs for sale! You even get to pick your own painted shells for them. They have shells with American flags and flowers and everything you can think of. My mom and dad won't let me get one. But I keep asking over and over, just in case they change their minds.

Our villa is just across the street from the beach. Well, actually it's called the sound, but that's pretty much the same thing. I can just barely see it from our balcony and I am DYING to go! I can't wait to see the dolphins. They hang out in the sound and just swim all around you. It makes me feel so happy.

I beg my parents to let me go down to the beach even though they aren't finished unpacking the car. And you know what? This time they said yes. You see? That's why you have to keep asking and asking for things. Eventually your parents get tired and just say okay.

My dad takes me and Mikey across the street just as the sun is setting. I speed ahead because I'm finally going to get to see my dolphin friends!

I make my way down the beach, watching the crabs with those big pinchers skitter away from my giant footsteps. I take extra care to hop around those freaky jellyfish that lay in blobs blocking my way like an obstacle course. Wouldn't want to step on one of those! Ouchie!

I wiggle my toes in the water and wait to see the first dolphin fin pop out of the sound. I wait. And wait. And wait.

"Do you see any dolphins, Dad?" I ask.

"Not yet, Maddie."

"Where are they?"

"I'm not sure, but we need be getting back. We can try again tomorrow."

It's getting dark and there are no lights along the beach to help us find our way back. That's on purpose. They can't keep lights on because the sea turtles lay their eggs on the beach here. When the babies hatch, they follow the moon to find their way back to the ocean. If there are lights along the edge of the beach, the hatchlings head towards those instead of the moon and never make it to the water. Very sad.

But I really want to wait for the dolphins because I KNOW they are coming. It's getting darker and my dad is insisting we get back inside before it's totally black. I try to stall because I just don't understand. Where are they?

*
* *
    *

6

The Perfect Sign

The first night sleeping in a new room that's not my room at home is always a little tricky. Number one, the bed is not my bed. And I've worked very hard to get my bed EXACTLY RIGHT. Number two is all the strange noises in the middle of the night.

Yeah, my house has strange noises, too, but not THESE noises. And even though I don't really know what a three-headed wolf monster creeping around a beach villa in the middle of the night actually sounds like, when it's three o'clock in the morning and you're in a strange bed, everything sounds like a three-headed wolf monster creeping around your beach villa. That is exactly why I spent the second half of the night with the covers pulled over my head.

And that is also exactly why I'm glad it's now morning! Plus, now the fun can really begin.

Guess what we're doing tonight? We're going to see Gregg Russell! Next to swimming in the ocean near the dolphins, going to see him is probably my most favorite part of the trip, and we're getting to do it on the first night! He sits under a huge tree just in front of the fancy yachts in Harbour Town. All the kids sit right on the stage with him.

As part of the show, he picks kids to come up to the microphone and sing a song. Now, I love to sing, so naturally I want to get picked to sing for the audience. The problem is, so does almost every other kid there.

But I did sing once. When I was FOUR. But now I'm TEN, and if you know how to do math you know that means I've gone five straight years without getting picked to sing! So this year, I just gotta get picked.

That brings me to my sign. You see, if you've been to the show before, you know that the kids who bring a sign to hold up are more likely to get picked.

I know these things because my Dad has been going to see Gregg Russell sing here since he was a kid.

And since it's taking my parents FOREVER to drink their coffee and get dressed this morning, I'm going to start on my sign. This year my mom brought glitter pens and sparkly gemstones for me to use on my sign, so it will definitely be my best one ever.

"Gregg Russell, you're my favorite singer!" I write on my sign. It's good to butter him up a little so he'll want to pick you. "Please pick me to sing" is what I write underneath. I load the edges with the sparkly decorations to catch his eye.

"Okay guys, who's ready to swim?" my Dad asks as I glue the last diamond to the bottom corner of my sign. Perfect.

"Me, me, me, me, me, me!" Mikey and I say together.

"I said it first!" taunts Mikey. "No I did!" I say, although I have no idea why I'm even arguing about this.

"No, I'm the winner, I get to go swimming!" Mikey screeches as loud as he can.

"Don't be silly, guys. We're all going swimming. It's not a competition," grumbles my dad.

Exactly. I know Mikey just does that to annoy me anyways. He's like the world's expert at that.

*
*   *
*

7

Strange Waters

"Ready, set, GO!" shouts my mom. We uncover our eyes and dip our faces into the water looking for the diving sticks she tossed all around the pool. After they sink to the bottom, it's a race to see who can collect the most.

This is a game I play with my dad. Mikey doesn't usually play because he doesn't like to swim to the bottom of the pool to get the sticks. Besides, most of the time he's trying to spray people with his long-range water squirter.

My dad and I always have fun playing our game, even though he never lets me win. Sometimes I win on my own. And sometimes while Dad is under the water, my mom secretly points out dive sticks she's hidden in places like the hot tub.

My mom is in the pool today only because the one at our villa is heated. Even though it's June and pretty sweaty outside, she always says it's too cold to get in the water otherwise. So crazy!

Just as dad and I cover our eyes for mom to toss out the next round, I get a big gush of pool water right in my face! "MIKEY!!!!" I am so frustrated with him. He knows he's not supposed to squirt faces, but he still does -- MINE!

"That's enough, you two," my dad sighs. "Maybe a change of scenery would help. Who wants to go to the beach?"

Sounds good to me. I still haven't seen any dolphins.

I wonder if my mom will come because the water is so much colder there, but she does. She likes to take pictures of us on the beach.

We all have to carry something. We have four neon towels, castle-shaped buckets, about five shovels, two sand chairs and a big blue umbrella. After we lug it all across the street to the beach, Mikey yells out, "Race!"

I almost trip racing him to the water. I don't know why Mikey thinks he has to be first. We splash in at about the same time. Okay, he may have been one toe ahead, but I'll never tell him that.

As soon as I hit the water, I notice something seems very different. It's the water. It's so WARM -- way warmer than the heated pool. At first I thought Mikey peed in the water again, but I don't really think he did.

Just to be sure, I walk a few feet away from him. It's still super warm. Strange.

8

Close Encounters

"Okay, Maddie Mack, don't go out any further than that!" my dad yells from the shoreline.

I always try to go out as far as I can when I swim in the ocean. I know it makes my parents nervous, but I also know it gives me a better chance of seeing a dolphin up close.

Only so far, no luck. Not one single dolphin. I've been out here for over an hour, and usually I would've seen several by now.

I know most everyone loves dolphins. They're cute and playful, and they're super smart. Some people think they're just as smart as people. I like them for all those reasons, too, but I also like them because I feel different when I'm around them. Whenever they're near me, all happy and playful, I feel happy and playful too. Like I can FEEL what they're feeling.

I told my family about this once, that it seems like I can feel what the dolphins are feeling. My mom and dad chuckled a little and said they thought that was cute, but I know they really didn't believe me. And Mikey made fun of me, of course. But I still believe it's true. That's why I want to see one so badly!

Just as I am about to call it quits and go work on my alligator sand castle, I spot it. Out of the corner of my eye, for just a split second, I'm almost certain I see a dolphin fin poke out of the water.

I fix my gaze to the spot where I think I saw it. And I wait.

There it is again! Only this time it's gotten even closer! When I see its fin come out of the water, I realize that this isn't a grown-up dolphin. Its fin is too small. It can't be more than two or three years old.

It pokes through the water one more time, and this time I can tell for sure that it's swimming right towards me! It's got the cutest little pattern of freckles on its dorsal fin.

I try my best to stay perfectly still so I don't give it any reason to change its mind. And trust me, being still has never been my strong suit. Just ask my teacher. But for a chance to get up close to a dolphin, I'll do anything.

Be calm, Maddie. Be calm. But where did it go? I haven't seen it pop up from the water for about a... oh my gosh, it's right in front of my face! A little nose lifts out of the water and our faces couldn't be more than a foot apart! This is amazing!!!

I want to scream and tell my family there's a dolphin right here in front of me, but I don't dare, because the last thing I want to do is scare the little guy away.

And I was right, too. This is definitely not a grown-up dolphin. The strange thing is, I've never seen a dolphin this small away from its mother. But I haven't spotted her anywhere.

Okay, now I want to touch him. Like really, really bad. I reach my arm out ever so slowly. Slowly. And... I'm touching his nose, I'm touching his nose! I can't believe no one in my family has noticed any of this yet.

The strange thing is, when I touch his nose, even though I'm super excited and I should be bursting with joy, I actually feel a little bit sad. What in the world?

The dolphin dives back into the water and I can see him just underneath the surface. He starts swimming in a little circle around me. He even keeps bumping into my leg, just like Butterpaws and Fluffles do when they greet me!

He looks up at me, and it almost seems like he's trying to tell me something. Unfortunately, I don't speak dolphin, so I have no idea what it is.

After circling around me a few more times, he starts to swim away. I was hoping he'd never leave, but I guess he probably has to get back to his mother. Maybe him sneaking this far away makes his parents nervous, too.

As he swims away, I feel a little confused. I mean, I pet a wild dolphin in the middle of the ocean, which is quite possibly the most amazing thing that's ever happened to me. That should've made me happier than I've ever felt before. So why in the world did I feel sad?

I stand there in the water for a few minutes trying to make sense of everything that just happened, when it occurs to me: I wasn't the one who was sad. The dolphin was sad. I know my family doesn't believe I can feel what they feel, but after this, I know it has to be true.

But if it is true, then why was the dolphin so sad?

9

Harbour Town

"I got you! You're out!" I tagged him. I really did. Mikey darts through the palm fronds at the South Beach Marina while my parents finish eating dinner. I wish I could meet a friend to play with instead because Mikey likes to cheat and say that I didn't really tag him out. Oh, brother. Literally.

But I guess it's tradition. Since our villa is right next to the marina, we usually eat here at the Salty Dog at least once each trip. You can eat outside at picnic tables and listen to a guy with a guitar playing old songs that my parents sing along to. Okay, that part is kind of gross.

THE LEGEND OF THE DOLPHIN LOCKET

After we eat, we usually get ice cream. Not tonight. Tonight we are saving that particular treat for Harbour Town. We catch the Sea Pines trolley and ride over with our hair blowing in our faces.

It's almost Gregg Russell time! We usually get to the show super early because my parents like to sit right in the front. That's so they can take a video if I get picked to sing. But it's been a looooong time since they have needed that camera!

We leave my dad to save the front bench at the show while we go with my mom to get melty cookie-dough ice cream from one of my favorite shops here -- the Cinnamon Bear. They have way more than ice cream. They have the next best thing to real live animals. Stuffed animals!

We also wander through Planet Hilton Head and the toy store. Did you see all that cool stuff? Geez, don't tell my mom, but I think she was right. I shouldn't have used all my money last week to buy a

Furby because now I wish I had money to buy that silvery-gray dolphin stuffie!

Oh well. I'm sure I can talk my grandma into buying me something before we leave. She can't resist when I give her a giant squeeze and say, "Puh-leeeeeease!!!!"

I'm looking through all the seashell bracelets and shark's tooth necklaces, looking for one with my name. It's hard to find stuff with my name on it. It would be so much easier if my name was Emma or Sophia.

Before I can finish looking, Mikey starts whining because he doesn't like to shop, so we have to stop and take him to see the lighthouse instead. Really? Who doesn't like shopping?

But the lighthouse is cool, too. It's right at the edge of the harbor and you can go all the way to the top. It's a lot taller than it looks. You figure that out fast when you start to climb the 114 steps. Phew!

The sun is going down and I'm getting anxious to grab my spot on the stage for the show. I race back down the steps before my mom even makes it all the way up to the top of the lighthouse. I quickly crunch through the crushed-shell walkway to get back to the stage.

I have to think about where I'm going to sit. I want to be right up front so Gregg Russell will notice me and won't forget about me this time. I pick out the exact spot I want, but then I see a girl who looks about my age and sit next to her instead.

A friend!

10

Ear-buds

"Hi! I'm Maddie," I say.

She doesn't say anything, just keeps looking straight in front of her. Hmm, that's strange. It kinda seems like she's ignoring me.

"Excuse me, what's your name?" I try again.

Still nothing. Still looking straight ahead.

Most kids might give up and move on by now. Not me. Making new friends is one of my specialties. I'm also very persistent. Just ask my parents.

I decide to try a new approach. I tap her on the left shoulder.

Success! She turns towards me and smiles a big, friendly smile. Then she reaches towards her ears and pulls out her... earbuds. Duh. No wonder she couldn't hear me! She pauses the music on her iPod.

"Hi," she says shyly, "I was just listening to some music. Sometimes I get a little lost in my own world when I do that."

"That happens to me, too!" I say. "I'm Maddie."

"I'm Samantha. But you can call me Sam."

"So have you ever seen the Gregg Russell show before?" I ask.

"No, this is my first time. Have you?"

"This is my tenth time. Although I don't remember the first couple."

"Is it good?"

"Oh my gosh, it's better than good! It's one of my favorite things to do in Hilton Head."

"Is it just songs and stuff?" Sam asks.

"There'll be some songs, and some really funny jokes, like when he makes fun of the parents. And throughout the show he picks kids to come up to the microphone and sing."

"I love to sing!" Sam's eyes get big.

"Me too! He picked me to sing once before when I was four, but he hasn't picked me again since. I just keep trying."

"What song do you sing when you go up there?"

"You get to pick," I tell her.

"Oh, I know exactly what I would sing," she says. "It's the song I was just listening to on my iPod. What do you want to sing, Maddie?"

"'Miss Movin' On' by Fifth Harmony," I tell her.

Sam's eyes get wide again. "What is it?" I ask.

She picks up her earbuds and sticks them in my ear. "Listen," she tells me excitedly.

She hits the play button on her iPod.

"Ah!" I shout, "It's 'Miss Movin' On'!"

"Fifth Harmony is my favorite group," Sam says.

"Mine too!" This has the makings of a very good friendship.

"So, how do you get picked?" she asks.

"Well, you raise your hand when he asks for volunteers. But there are things you can do to make it more likely you'll get picked. Like making a really great sign."

"A sign?" Sam looks puzzled.

"Yeah, in just a bit he'll ask all the kids to hold up their signs. And then he'll walk around and read every single one. Here's mine."

I show Sam my sign. "I think this is my best one yet. I really, really hope it works!"

"Wow, that looks so cool," Sam says, touching the gemstones. "So sparkly!"

"Thanks!"

"I don't have a sign. I guess that means I probably won't get picked. Oh well."

I can tell from the look on her face that, even though she's trying her best not to show it, Sam's a little disappointed she didn't know about the sign thing.

11

Sacrifice

"Okay kids, let me see your signs," Gregg Russell finally announces after singing a few songs.

He moves to the other end of the stage and starts reading them aloud one by one.

You can tell that a lot of the signs were made at the last minute. One kid wrote his on a napkin, and his little brother used the back of a pizza box.

Then he gets to a little girl who has a neon-orange poster-board sign. He reads it out loud: "I love you, Gregg Russell. Tonight is my last night in Hilton Head." Ooh, that's a good one. Competition.

He's getting closer to me. I can feel my heart beating faster. I always get really nervous right before he reads my sign.

I look over at Sam and see she has the same disappointed look she had earlier. And I'm pretty sure I know why.

The kid right in front of us is holding up a paper plate. As Gregg Russell starts to read the message on it, I lean over to Sam. "Here," I say, trying to give her my sign. "You hold it up."

Sam looks surprised. "What? Why?" she questions.

"This is your first time here. I've gotten to sing before and you never have."

"Your dad helped you with that sign, didn't he, Junior Pants?" Gregg Russell says to the kid with paper plate.

"Are you sure, Maddie?" Sam asks. Gregg Russell is heading right for us.

"Definitely! Here, take it quick." I shove the sign into her hands. Sam timidly raises it over her head real quick.

"Oooh," Gregg Russell says. "Jewels and glitter pens. Dad had no part in the making of this sign, did he?" He puts the microphone in front of Sam, waiting for a response. She doesn't exactly know what to say.

"Uh, no," she giggles. "Actually, I..."

"Gregg Russell, you're my favorite singer," he reads. "Please pick me!"

"You worked really hard on that. I can tell. Remember to raise your hand up real high when I ask for volunteers to sing. Okay?" Sam nods her head.

After he moves away, she looks over at me with a big smile on her face, and whispers "Thank you, Maddie."

"Of course!" I reply. Like I said, nothing beats making a new friend.

12

Duet

Okay, I'm starting to chew on my nails here. Not many more kids will get picked. Gregg Russell has to save time to sing his own songs. He's already chosen the girl who's leaving tomorrow and that kid who wrote his sign on the back of a pizza box. I think he felt sorry for him.

Here's the thing: Gregg Russell alternates between picking boys and girls and he usually asks the littlest kids to sing because they say silly things that make the adults in the audience laugh. That means neither Sam nor I have a great shot, but we're still raising our hands as tall as we can reach while our fingers wiggle-waggle to get his attention.

This time he picks a set of four-year old twins and they forget what song they were going to sing. Gregg Russell gets a big laugh from the audience when he tries to help them figure out what songs they both know. Maybe that means he'll get to a big kid next.

After the twins muddle their way through the ABCs, Gregg Russell calls, "We've got time for ONE more!" Oh, it just has to be Sam or me!

I almost can't decide which I'd like more. I mean, I really want to sing, but I'd like my new friend to get to sing also.

As Gregg Russell searches for his next performer, I look at Sam and see on her face how much she wants this, too. And when I look back up to the front, I can see that he's zeroed in on HER!

I am bursting with excitement for Sam. And maybe a little bit sad, too.

She glances at me to make sure it's okay, but I only show her my happiest face and wave her up. At the microphone, she answers questions about her age and where she's from.

When Gregg Russell asks if she's ready to sing, she looks down at the floor and slowly shakes her head. What? Surely she isn't going to chicken out!

Nope. Instead, she points right at ME and tells Gregg Russell that she can't sing the song without her friend. "Ooohhh, alright," he agrees. "Let's get her up here quick!"

I hop over a few kids and bounce up to the microphone next to Sam. We look at each other with smiles so big our cheeks hurt, take a deep breath and start, "I'm breakin' down, gonna start from scratch. Shake it off like an Etch-a-sketch..."

A friend!

13

False Accusations

I couldn't sleep at all last night. But this time it wasn't the three-headed wolf monster that kept me awake, it was thinking about how awesome the Gregg Russell concert was. I FINALLY got to sing again on stage AND I made a great new friend. Speaking of my new friend, I really hope I get a chance to see Sam again while we're here.

This morning it's Forest Preserve time! I love it there. It's huge, and nobody is allowed to build things on it. So everything there still probably looks like it did a thousand years ago, except for a few bridges and stuff.

And there are so many animals, including lots of swamps with alligators and TONS of turtles.

There's also this big ring of oyster shells inside the forest -- the Shell Ring. They say the Native Americans who used to live here 4000 years ago made it, and probably had celebrations or ceremonies inside of it. That's so cool.

We always bike over to the forest at least once while we're here, and that's what we're doing this morning.

"Don't get too far ahead of us, Maddie Mack!" my dad yells from behind me. I love to pedal really fast on the bike paths, but, of course, this makes my parents nervous. So, just like in the ocean, I usually keep going until they yell for me to stop.

I know my way to the Forest Preserve, anyhow. Mikey just learned how to ride his bike without training wheels, so we're having to go even slower than usual. Maddie Mackenzie doesn't do slow!

We usually go through the Lawton entrance to the Forest Preserve, because it's closer to our villa in South Beach. So we have to pass through the Hilton Head Preparatory School parking lot to get there. School must be out here, too, because the parking lot is empty, and there aren't any kids outside playing.

I speed up ahead again and race towards the entrance to the forest. I hop off my bike and put down the kickstand.

I look behind me and see Mikey turning into the school entrance. "Looking good, Mikey!" I yell. He's riding in between my mom and dad. "You're doing great!" I remember I felt a little nervous on the bike paths after first learning how to ride my bike, so I thought he might like the encouragement.

They ride up to where I'm standing at the entrance to the forest. Dad chains our bikes onto the rack, and off we go down the forest path.

"Now don't get dirty yet, guys," my mom pleads. She's got her nice camera with her. "I want some good pictures."

Mom always takes pictures of us here. That's the part Mikey and I like the least. I don't mind doing my fashion model poses, but mom says I'm supposed to "look natural."

We walk down the forest trail together until we hit a split in the path. "We can keep going straight and head down the 'Shell Ring Trail,'" my dad says, "or we can turn left and go down the Fish Island Trail."

"Shell Ring!" I shout.

"Fish Island!" Mikey yells. I know he just said that 'cause I chose the Shell Ring. Grrr.

"Well, while we're deciding, why don't we take some pictures!" my mom suggests.

Oh man, we walked right into that one.

"Okay, Maddie and Mikey, how about you guys stand right in front of that big moss-covered oak tree there."

Mikey and I do as mom says, trying to get the picture taking over as quickly as we can. We stand side by side in front of the tree.

"Now, smile guys," mom says. We both give our best "cheese" smiles, hoping she will just click one picture and be done. Of course, it's never that easy.

"Okay, how about you two hold hands now?" mom asks.

"What?!" Mikey protests. "Gross!"

"Come on, Mikey. Let's just do it so we can keep exploring the forest," I plead.

VACATION ADVENTURE GIRL #1

I grab Mikey's hand. Mom snaps a few pictures of us with our hands together. Then I start to hear Mikey giggle a little bit under his breath. He's up to something, I know.

He starts squeezing my hand harder. I try not to notice or do anything, 'cause I just want to get done with the pictures and get back to exploring. But he keeps on squeezing. It starts to hurt, and I know I can't keep my hand in his much longer.

Finally, I can't take it and I yank my hand away. I end up pulling so hard I stumble and fall into mom, making her drop her camera.

"Maddie!" she gasps. "Why on earth did you do that?"

"It wasn't me," I explain. "Mikey made me do that."

"Maddie Mack, don't blame your brother," dad says. "He was just standing there. This wasn't his fault."

"But he was squeezing my hand really hard," I explain. I'm trying not to cry, but I can feel the tears welling up in my eyes.

"I'm always getting blamed for stuff that's not my fault. And he's always getting away with things just because he's younger. It's not fair!" Now I'm crying. So much for holding back the tears.

"Sometimes I wish I could live with another family," I yell.

You know how sometimes when you get really upset and frustrated you say or do things that you don't really mean? And even as you're saying and doing them you wish you could stop yourself and take them back, but it's too late. Well that's kind of how I feel about that last thing I said.

I really don't want to live with another family. But that's what I said. And I'm so upset, and so ashamed for saying it, that I find myself running down the Shell Ring trail. I just want to be alone for a minute.

14

A Whole New World

Whoa! Look at that flower -- glowing fluorescent orange with green, glittery sparkles like miniature emeralds shooting out of it. I've never seen anything like that here. Or anywhere else, for that matter. I drew a picture of it in my journal to show Mikey and my parents:

I kneel down to examine it. It looks so fragile, like it might dissolve into emerald dust if I touch it. While I look at it, I almost forget about the ugly words I said to my family. Almost. At least it helps me take my mind off them. I wish I had my phone so I could take a picture of this flower, but my drawing will have to do.

I guess I'd better get going before my parents start to worry. I'd better go apologize. Maybe they will forget about my tantrum when I bring them back here to see these amazing flowers! That will distract them.

But as I stand up, I notice that there are a few more of the glowing flowers ahead. They line the path that shoots off the one I was taking to the Shell Ring. I'm sure I've never seen THAT path before. I would remember these fluorescent flowers.

I decide to take a few steps down the path just to see where it goes. As soon as I step off the main Shell Ring path, I pass through a ray of sunshine peeking through the treetops. It's like a shimmery curtain that sparkles like those flowers. It's like... magic.

I glide right through this wonder of light and find myself in a very strange, but beautiful, place I've never seen before. Am I still in the Forest Preserve?

And look! The colors of the all the plants here are so bright and cheerful and very different from any I've seen before in the forest. I wander down the path, unable to make myself go back yet. I've just got to see more of this place! Oh, why don't I have my camera with me?

A buzzing sound catches my attention and I squat down to examine something that looks a little like a venus fly trap. The buzzing grows louder the closer I get. The whole plant is shaking and humming. What in the world?

I lean in a little closer and just as I do -- POP! It bursts open with a sound so loud that I jump and almost fall over. But I'm curious, so I can't help but creep closer to look at this crazy thing.

What is that? Yash! Look! There's something shiny inside -- deep down inside the stem. I can just see it. Something like an oyster shell, kind of like the ones with pearls inside. But this shell is more pearly on the outside. Why would a shell be inside a plant? Weird. What's even weirder is that the plant is still humming and buzzing and leaning towards me like it wants me to take the shell.

Should I touch it? I wonder what would happen if I do.

I hold my breath and make a quick grab for the shell. Got it! I'll put it back. I just want to look at it for a minute.

I let my breath out as I uncurl my fingers to peek at the treasure inside. Immediately the plant stops buzzing and seems to wilt. I hope I didn't hurt it. But it seemed like it wanted me to take the shell. So strange!

I can hear something rattling inside the pearly shell. Ooohh! I wonder what's inside! It seems very delicate, so I try to open the shell very gently. But it's locked up tight. I really want to get it open, so I poke my fingers between the two halves to pry them apart, but it still won't budge. I'm looking around looking for a tiny stick or something to use to wedge it open and I notice something else puzzling. It's glowing!

All of the sudden, the edges start to light up and send off those shooting sparkles like the flowers, but this time a purply color. Uh oh, I think there might be something still alive inside this thing!

I notice the glow starts to change and there are some very faint markings like little shadows on the shell. I rub my fingers over the markings and they get brighter, now a brighter purply blue than the rest of the shell. But I can't figure out what they are, except one that looks a little like a dolphin. They remind me of those Egyptian hieroglyphics Ms. Applebottom taught us about.

Shloouptck! Wha...? The shell makes a funny vacuum-like noise and just slurps open. It opens on its own? Now I can see what's rattling inside.

You won't believe this. It's a dolphin! A necklace with a blue dolphin locket on it. And it is AWESOME. It's this small blue dolphin that looks like it just leapt out of the water.

And I don't know why, because it isn't mine, but I am just DYING to put it on. I gently lift it out of the shell, which is still glowing those purple pictures, by the way.

My mom always helps me put my necklaces on because I can never get them to attach, but she's not here. So I just hold it up to my neck to see what it might look like on me. But before I can grab hold of the clasp, something incredible happens. It attaches itself! I don't even need my mom to clip it together!

I look down at the dolphin hanging from my neck and it seems to glow like the flowers and the shell. Am I in a dream?

15

Lost

O kay, so nothing this strange and amazing has ever happened to me before. A venus fly trap plant thingy hands me a glowing shell containing a beautiful dolphin locket that magically clasps itself around my neck! The locket is so pretty that I must've been standing here staring at it for 30 minutes, running it through my fingers. But then I snap out of it and think: Where is my family?

I'm pretty sure I've been gone for nearly an hour. I thought surely my family would have come running after me when I stormed off like that, but I guess I was wrong. Maybe they're trying to teach me a lesson by ignoring me.

At this point, I don't care. I just want to see them. Even more, I want to tell them about the flowers and show them the locket. I turn around and start running back the way I came, only... I can't seem to find the way I came. Nothing in this forest looks familiar anymore. I have no idea how to get back.

I start to panic.

"Mom!" I yell. "Dad! Mikey!" Yes, I'd even settle for seeing Mikey at this point.

No answer. Just the sound of the birds chirping and the wind rustling through the treetops. It's way too quiet here.

I call again, "Mom!" I wait.

"Mom!" yells another voice off in the distance. "Dad!" the other voice says.

It sounds like someone else is echoing me. How strange.

"Hello!" I say, and wait.

"Hello!" says the other voice.

I start heading in the direction of the sound. "Stay there," I say, "I'm coming to you." I walk towards where I heard the sound coming from.

"Okay," the other voice replies. I can tell that I'm definitely getting closer. And I can tell that the other voice is definitely from a girl.

I keep heading in the direction of the voice until I finally catch a glimpse of some dark, black hair woven into a French braid. It's clearly the back of a little girl's head. I start to run towards her. She hears me and turns around. Hey! I know that face!

"Sam!" I scream. "Maddie!" she shouts back.

"What are you doing here?!" I ask.

"I don't really know," she replies. "I'm not even sure where we are. I was walking with my family in the Forest Preserve and then I got a little curious about this path off to the side and decided to explore. Next thing I knew, I was surrounded by all sorts of crazy looking plants and fluorescent flowers."

"Me too!" I exclaim. "I don't know what this place is. I've been coming to the Sea Pines Forest Preserve for years and have never seen anything like it."

"I'm getting scared, Maddie," Sam whispers. "Where are our parents?"

"I know," I reply. "I'm sure we'll find them." The truth is, I'm not at all sure, but I don't want her to be scared.

"Whoa!" Sam gasps. "Where did you get that?!" She points to my dolphin locket.

"From a plant!" I start giggling.

"A what?!" She looks very confused.

"Yeah, this plant reached out and just handed me this shell, and I took it, and then these strange marks started to glow, and the shell popped open, and then there was this dolphin locket inside, and it flew out and clasped itself around my neck," I said without taking a breath.

"Ooooookay," Sam says. Now she looks even more confused. "It's soooo beautiful." She reaches out and touches it.

"I know."

"And what about those little creatures with the mushrooms on their head?" she asks.

"Huh?" I reply. Now I'm the one who's confused.

"You haven't seen them?" Sam asks. "I saw one, but as soon as I turned to look at it, it scampered off behind a tree."

"What did it look like?" I ask.

"It was actually kinda cute. Maybe about two feet tall. And it was either wearing a mushroom hat or had a mushroom for a head. Really big eyes."

"Whoa!"

"Yeah, I've never seen anything like it before."

All of the sudden, I get the feeling that we're being watched. I turn around and, sure enough, from behind a tree, I see two giant eyes peeking out at us, just like Sam described.

"Sam! Look!" I try to whisper. But I'm way too excited and it comes out as kind of a shout. The little mushroom guy hears me, turns around and starts running the other way.

"Follow it!" we both say together.

*

16

Found

Sam and I crouch down low and scurry to try to keep up with the little thing. Boy, it's fast! We are trying to dart between trees so that it doesn't see us. But everything is so quiet around here, it will probably hear us crunching through the dried leaves and pinestraw even if it doesn't see us.

I really want to get a closer look at this guy. It's kind of like a little person. Or an animal. Or both. I'm not really sure. Its fingers and toes look kind of stubby, like a cross between paws and hands. Maybe it's a little person because it seems to be wearing clothes -- that mushroom hat plus a little vest made of leaves woven together and these short pants that look like they might be made of bark.

As it passes between trees, the sun glints off of something hanging from a string of miniature shells around its neck. A locket maybe? Or some sort of charm.

Oh! It stopped. Sam and I slip behind a scraggly bush to hide. Sam is glancing around and I realize that we've been so focused on this little creature that we haven't paid any attention to where we came from. I know she's thinking the same thing.

And just as suddenly as we stopped, we're moving again, trying to follow the mushroom guy. We sneak our way through a thick patch of bushes and come to a clearing that feels a little bit familiar. Maybe I've been here before. We stay at the edge, still hidden in the brush. We see a large circular clearing, surrounded by a continuous mound of buried shells.

The Shell Ring! I knew I recognized this place!

But, wait. It's different. Something's happening here. There are TONS of those little mushroom guys! They are all singing or kind of chanting the same sounds. And they are positioned in groups all around this giant fire in the middle of the ring.

Each group takes turns performing a dance around the fire while the rest of the creatures keep rhythm with their chant. I'm not sure what's going on, but it seems like it's important.

The little guys all have those little shell string necklaces and the mushroom hats, but some are different shapes and colors. And each grouping seems to be dressed just a little differently.

Man, if I ever needed my phone to take a picture, it's NOW!

Sam and I glance at each other and she looks just as surprised as I feel. And just then the chanting stops and all becomes silent. We turn back to look at the gathering and find ourselves looking right into the eyes of one of the creatures.

Then I see that there are maybe a dozen of them surrounding us and they don't look happy.

Um, so I think we might have a problem here.

* * *

17

A Royal Welcome

The last time my best friend Jessica and I had a breath-holding contest at school, I think my record was 27 seconds. Just now, as Sam and I glanced back to see all those forest creatures with their big eyes fixed right on us, I bet I beat my record by about two minutes.

And I'm pretty sure Sam isn't breathing either.

I have no idea if these guys are friendly, or if they're about to roast us over the fire and serve us up for dinner. I have never seen such creatures before.

It sort of seems as if they are as surprised to see us as we are to see them. After staring at us for what seems like forever, one of them steps forward and grabs each of us by an arm. He's a good bit smaller than we are, and his stubby hands are barely big enough to get a grip on us. He's not rough, but he's determined to take us somewhere.

After a few steps, he pauses to talk to the rest of his friends. He sounds angry, but I can't understand what he's saying. He's definitely not speaking English. The whole group of mushroom guys join in, all jabbering at once. They sound as if they're arguing, and their voices are getting louder and louder. That continues for several minutes until one of them looks at me bug-eyed and lets out a huge gasp. He's pointing at my neck.

They all go silent.

They're looking at me. Well, not exactly. They're looking at my neck.

The locket! They see my dolphin locket. I'm not sure why, but for whatever reason, seeing it has made them all stop arguing. Maybe it belongs to them. Oh no!

They gather around me in a semicircle and I frantically try to explain, "Wait. I didn't... I didn't mean to take it! There was this plant, and it reached out and handed me this shell, and out came this necklace, and it clasped around my neck all by itself, and..."

But before I can finish explaining, they all begin to kneel and bow their heads.

Are they bowing to me? Like I'm a queen or something? Ok, weird.

"Maddie, what's going on?" Sam looks as confused as I feel.

"I have no idea! But at least they stopped arguing. And it seems like they aren't going to eat us," I whisper to her.

One of the creatures approaches me. He looks like he's a bit older than the others. He extends his wide hand with his palm facing the sky. I think he wants me to take it.

Slowly, I reach for it, worried about what's happening. His hand is so small that it seems to disappear in mine.

He turns away from me and starts walking, pulling me by the hand. I wonder where he's leading us. "Sam, come with us," I urge, and Sam follows along. We gingerly pick our way through some thick bushes since we are much bigger and don't fit through the narrow spaces as easily.

We come to a circular clearing: the Shell Ring. And now, instead of a dozen of these little guys quietly staring at us, there are HUNDREDS. The chanting and dancing has stopped and it's really, really quiet. All I can hear is the loud popping and crackling of the giant blaze of fire in the center of the ring. I wonder if the mushroom guy holding my hand has noticed that it's getting sweaty since I'm so nervous.

The little guy steps in front of me and says something to the group assembled around the fire in the Shell Ring. He gestures to my neck and as soon as he does, something crazy happens. They all begin dropping to their knees and bowing their heads, just like the others did. Why do they keep doing that?

Before I can begin to think about what's happening, he's pulling me forward again. He leads me through the middle of the ring, by the fire and past all of the kneeling mushroom people. We're heading towards a little staircase that leads to a hut made out of mud, twigs and palm fronds.

We climb the tiny steps and stop at the top in front of a door made of twigs woven together with twine. The top of it comes to about my shoulders. I'm not sure I want to know what's on the other side. I can see glimpses of the hut's interior between the door's twigs, but I can't make out much through the darkness.

The little guy opens the door and heads in. I have to duck to keep from smacking my head. Sam follows through behind me. I'm so glad she's here, but where is he taking us?

*
* *
* *

18

The Chosen One

Inside, I am able to stand a little taller but I have to stop a moment to let my eyes adjust to the dark room. The only light in here is from a few clay pots with tiny fires in the middle. The pots are small enough to hold in the palm of my hand.

Someone must live here. There are little stumps and logs carved into furniture and an area that looks like a little kitchen with stacks of clamshells that would make perfect little soup bowls for these guys.

I see another one of the creatures sitting on some fur and looking at us. He's watching me as I check out the hut. He looks older than the rest of them and has a concerned, and kind of sad, look on his face.

He holds out an arm and waves it at a small mat made from intricately woven palm fronds. I think he wants me to sit. I do and I notice that Sam sits on another mat across from me. The little creature lowers his eyes and gently bows his head towards me. I feel like I'm supposed to know what is happening, but I really don't.

He looks at me for a long time and I start to feel uncomfortable. Am I supposed to say something here? Do something? I look at Sam and she sort of shrugs.

"Thank you for coming. I am Gilbius, the leader of the Wapaho people. We have been waiting for you," he says slowly in a deep voice. I can understand him! I wonder if the others speak English, too?

Wait a sec, did he just say he has been waiting for ME?

I look at Sam and I know that she's just as confused as I am. He's got me mixed up with someone else. We look back at him, our wide eyes full of questions. But before I can start the asking, he continues, "Yes, we have been waiting for you. Our people, our animals and our island are all in great danger. The island's protectors, the dolphins, are leaving, and we don't know why. You are the only one that can save us. It is good that you have come now."

Um, I don't even know what to say here. He must be the one that's confused. He can't be talking about ME. I have to tell him right away. "Ummm, so I think... You don't know me..." He holds up his stubby hand to stop me. I stop talking.

He gives his head a little shake, "I know that necklace."

Oh no! I was right earlier. The dolphin necklace is theirs and they think I stole it! I knew I shouldn't have touched it! Maybe it's really valuable and they were hiding it in that plant!

"That necklace has a story, you see. Dolphins are important to our people and this island. For many years, we lived happily side-by-side with the first Native Americans who lived on these lands. They built this Shell Ring. That was very long ago.

"Legend has it that the tribal elders, using their ancient magic, could speak with the dolphins, who are also magical. They agreed to unite in using their special powers to keep the island safe. They forged this locket as a symbol of their bond, right here in the fire of the Shell Ring.

"When it came time for the tribe to move on, they filled the locket with their ancient magic, and hid it here on the island. The locket's magic could only be released if the island was in danger. The wearer of the locket would possess the magic of the elders, allowing him or her to speak with the dolphins and call upon their help."

"I understand," I said, interrupting Gilbius. "I've found the locket. And you guys want it back."

"It would do me no good," Gilbius replied.

"No good? Why not?"

"Because the necklace can only be worn by one person. And that person is you. The elders knew that the magic of the locket was a special responsibility, and required a special person. The locket will only reveal itself to a person who shares the traits of the dolphins: courage, loyalty, curiosity, and kindness. Someone who will put the needs of others above her own.

"The locket chose you, Maddie. You are the one who must save us and Hilton Head Island."

"Save you? Save you from what?"

"Fires are breaking out across the island, destroying the homes of so many of our animal brothers and plant sisters. As more dolphins leave the waters here, taking their magic with them, the fires grow stronger. We need you, Maddie, to use the power of the locket to find out why."

Whoa. This is so much to take in. The dolphins? The island's in trouble? Ancient magic? Me? What?

"We have been holding ceremonies around the Fire of Shell Ring for many moons to summon the wearer of the dolphin locket. You are finally here. You're our last hope."

"Save us, Maddie Mackenzie."

19

Courage

Whoa.

My head is spinning. I've heard my mom say that before -- "my head is spinning" -- and I never really knew what she was talking about.

But now I know. Everything around me seems like it's moving. Or wobbling around, at least. Maybe it should be "my head is wobbling." Either way, I don't feel too good. I can also feel my stomach churning around like I might barf.

As the same little guy that brought me leads me back out the hut and towards the Shell Ring, Gilbius's words keep echoing in my head: "The locket chose you, Maddie. You are the one who must save us and Hilton Head Island." How on earth am I supposed to save them? Did he happen to notice that I'm just a ten-year old girl from Atlanta?!

As we're led towards the outer edge of the Shell Ring, Sam leans over to me and whispers, "Maddie, this is so amazing and exciting."

Did she just say what I think she said?

"Amazing and exciting?!" I whisper too loudly to Sam. I think I startled a few of the mushroom guys, er, I mean Wapaho, because a bunch of them are now looking at me with their big green-and-brown-flecked eyes. I lower my voice, "Sam, clearly they've got this ALL wrong. There's no way I can save them."

"Clearly, they've got this all RIGHT, Maddie," Sam replies.

"Didn't you hear what Gilbius said back there? All that stuff about the traits of the dolphin? That's not me. They've got the wrong kid!"

"Oh yes, that totally is you." Sam grabs both my shoulders and turns me to face her. "Maddie," she says, "I've only known you for less than a day, but I already know all those things he said about you are true. You're super smart, you love to read and learn about the world around you."

"But..."

"I'm not finished," Sam says, interrupting my protest. "And, most importantly, you're an amazing friend. Last night, at the Gregg Russell concert, you GAVE ME YOUR SIGN. I know how much you wanted to get on stage, but you just gave me your chance to get up there. I don't know any other kid who would have done that, Maddie."

"But, Sam," I kind of whine, "I don't know how to save anyone. He said there are fires breaking out everywhere, and they're expecting me to figure out how to stop them?!"

"Look, Maddie, at this point it doesn't even matter whether you think he's wrong or right. They think you're the chosen one, and so does that locket. And now you have its powers."

I look up at Sam and give her a weak smile. She is making sense.

"Besides, Maddie, you love this place. You've told me how much Hilton Head means to you, especially the forest and the animals. And if this place is in danger, and you can help, then you have to try, right?"

Sam is right. I know I'm just feeling like this because I'm scared. I was just supposed to be going on a fun little walk through the forest with my family, and now the entire fate of Hilton Head is on my shoulders? I still don't quite understand how this all happened.

"You're right, Sam," I agree. "I do love this place. And I'll do anything I can to try to save it."

I then do something I do whenever I'm feeling a little nervous. I close my eyes and take a deep breath. Then I clench my hands together into fists and stomp my foot on the ground to give me extra courage.

"Okay," I say, trying to make my voice sound as strong as I can. "I'm ready."

* *
*

20

Firefighter

We step into the center of the Shell Ring by the roaring fire and stare out at all the little faces looking up at us. They seem like they're waiting for us to say or do something. It's a little freaky.

Thankfully, Gilbius comes to stand beside us and all those big eyes turn to look at him instead. He speaks to the group in a language that we don't understand, but I can tell he is talking about us from the way the eyes in the audience dart back and forth from him to us.

All of the sudden, Gilbius points directly at me. He gently lifts the dolphin locket to show it to the waiting crowd before us. I kind of nibble at my lip nervously and peek over at Sam. She's smiling and gives me an encouraging nod.

When I look back at the group, I see that they have silently dropped to one knee and have their heads bowed. They're doing it again.

I notice that Gilbius and Sam are bowing, too. And even though the fire is making my back hot, tiny little goosebumps pop out on my arms and legs. I take another deep breath.

Now there is a flurry of activity. The chanting has started again, even louder than before. Everyone starts to dance. It's obvious they're happy that I'm here. It's hard not to let myself smile a big, goofy grin.

Sam and I are led over to small tree stumps to sit on while we watch. Gilbius joins us on a tiny stump of his own. "Before, they were calling you," Gilbius explains. "Now, Maddie, they are celebrating your arrival."

I still have no idea what I'm supposed to be doing to help, so I just watch the festivities and tap my feet along to the rhythm of the chant. Sam and I giggle at the little jigs the Wapaho groups do. Was that a breakdancing move?

We hear a commotion nearby and shift to look around the fire to see what is happening. The celebration comes to a halt as dozens of deer, raccoons, rabbits, squirrels and other small animals rush into the Shell Ring. The animals don't look happy. I have a sinking feeling that my job here is about to begin, and that this has something to do with those fires we heard about.

Gilbius rushes forward to greet the animals and signals to the Wapaho tribe. A group wearing tiny owl necklaces and vests made of fur instead of woven leaves makes its way into the cluster of animals. Each Wapaho pairs with a different animal, placing a hand on its back and leaning in close.

"I think they are talking to the animals!" Sam whispers. She's right! This fur-wearing Wapaho group and the animals are all exchanging soft bleating sounds. It's fascinating.

Gilbius hears Sam and explains, "All the Wapaho have a role to play in our community. See the owl emblems that they wear around their necks? That is the mark of the animal whisperers. They communicate by sound and touch, and can sense what the animals are feeling."

He looks worried as he continues, "There have been more fires. All of these animals have lost their homes. They have come to seek shelter and to warn us that the fires are heading towards the Forest Preserve. Our forest friends have also seen more dolphins leaving their posts surrounding the island."

"Can't the animal whisperers just ask the dolphins why they are leaving?"

Gilbius shakes his head, "Our animal whisperers can only communicate with our forest neighbors, not with the sea life."

"But I can!" I shout, before realizing what I'm saying. Everyone stops to stare at me with wide eyes.

"I mean, now that I have the locket, I can talk to them, can't I?"

Gilbius and the animal whisperers nod at each other as another Wapaho approaches, this one dressed in all brown bark and wearing a necklace with an arrow emblem.

"This is Pipperdee, she is one of our island guides. You can call her Pip. She will lead you through the tunnels to the Sound, so you can meet with the remaining dolphins to find out what is going on."

I guess this is really happening.

Gilbius nods and the Wapaho all drop back to one knee. Pip waves her hand in the direction we're to head.

I grab Sam's hand and we follow.

21

Talking Dolphin

As Pipperdee leads us out of the Shell Ring and into the forest, I can tell that the forest animals were right. The fires are definitely getting worse, I smell them. From what I can see, it seems like it's only a matter of time before there's no forest left.

We're walking so fast, we're almost running. I think Pip knows that time is running out, too. We head down a little path that's been carved out by the Wapaho. The ground cover has been cleared away, but the plants and bushes have grown over the top of it, coming right over Pip's head.

This means that Sam and I have to duck down real low just to fit. As we snake our way through the path, I can feel a salty breeze on my face. We're heading towards the ocean.

Except it looks like our path is running out. We come to a big live oak tree that's sitting right in our way. I hope our guide knows where she's going.

All of a sudden, she drops to her knees and starts brushing away the leaves and sticks on the ground in front of us. What on earth is she doing?

"Maddie, look! A door!" Sam shrieks excitedly. I see it, too. A small, square door, covered with helicopter seeds, appears as Pip clears the area. It's made of branches and moss and in the center there's a small carving in the wood. It's the outline of a dolphin!

Pip pulls the handle and it swings upwards to reveal a tunnel underneath. "This way," she whispers.

She climbs down into the tunnel. She has to duck to walk through it, which means Sam and I have to crawl. It's dark in here, and I can't really see much of anything, so I'm doing my best to crawl as fast as I can to keep up with the sound of Pip's footsteps ahead. We must be ten feet underground here.

"Sam, look up there," I say, out of breath from crawling so quickly.

"Light!" Sam says. Up ahead, there's another little door on the roof of our tunnel, and sunlight is streaming through the cracks. In the distance, I can hear the sound of the waves crashing against the beach.

"This must be their secret tunnel to the ocean, Sam."

Pip comes to a stop and starts climbing up a little ladder on the wall. Sam heads up behind her. Just as I'm about to place my foot on the first rung of the ladder, I spot something flickering out of the corner of my eye.

I look closer and notice a cluster of tiny little holes in the wall of the tunnel. They're perfect little circles and they seem to glow from inside. Now that I've spotted them, I see that they're everywhere along the walls up and down the tunnels

"Hey, Pip, what are these for?" I ask. She looks down from the top of the ladder as I point towards the little holes. Pip shrugs. She doesn't know, but she doesn't seem to give it too much thought.

I try to stick my finger into one of the holes. Ouch! It's super hot. How strange.

"Maddie, come on!" Sam shouts from the top of the ladder.

"Okay, okay, coming," I climb up the ladder and out through the door and... it's so bright! I'm so blinded by the sun that it takes me a minute to realize I'm standing on the sand. The tunnel leads straight from the forest to the beach! Pip motions for us to come with her down to the water.

"Maddie, look at your locket!" Sam shrieks. "It's glowing brighter!"

I look down and see it, too. The entire outline of my dolphin locket is glowing a pinkish-purplish color. Then, all by itself, it lifts away from my chest and out in front of me. It's gently tugging on the cord around my neck, like it's leading me somewhere.

I follow. It's taking me into the ocean. And then, out in the distance, I see it. A little dolphin fin pokes out of the water for just a second, and then it's gone again. I keep watching until I see several dolphin fins poke out together. There are at least three of them, and they're coming right towards me.

I stand perfectly still because I don't really know what else to do. As they start to get closer, I can see their bodies under the water. Just as they're about to reach me, they all poke their heads out and come to a quick stop, spraying water into our faces. "Whoa," Sam laughs, "that was cool."

The dolphin in the middle opens its mouth and says, "We are so happy to see you." Then the one on its left says, "We thought you were never coming back."

Um, what just happened?

"Sam, these dolphins can talk!" I shriek.

"Um, they can talk dolphin, you mean." Sam replies.

"No, that was English! They can speak English!"

"Sounded like regular old dolphin sounds to me, Maddie."

I look down and see the locket is resting against my chest again, but glowing really bright. Oh right, the locket. I guess Sam can't understand them.

"My name is Maddie. Can you understand me, too?" I say to them.

They bob their heads up and down. "Yes, we can," says the one in the middle. He seems to be the spokesperson. "And we need your help."

"My help? I was coming to get you to help us!"

"A long time ago our great ancestors pledged to protect this island with our magic. And for thousands of years, we've kept that oath. But we cannot stay much longer."

"Why not? We don't understand."

"It's the water around the island. It has been getting warmer recently, and seems to be getting hotter every day. This has driven almost all the fish that we eat to swim away from Hilton Head. Most of the dolphins in our pod have already left the island to keep from starving. There are only a few of us left, and our magic is greatly weakened."

"Does this have anything to do with the wildfires in the forest?"

"We don't know. But we're counting on you to figure it out. We don't have much time," he tells me.

"But what if I can't? I mean, I'll try, but you know I'm just a little girl, right?

"You are the chosen one, Maddie. The locket believes in you, and so do we.

22

Detective

It seems like too much of a coincidence that the waters are warming at the same time the wildfires are spreading. I just know they have to be connected.

I'm so focused on trying to figure out the connection that I almost wander in the wrong direction. I have my head down, thinking hard as I walk, when Sam grabs my elbow, "Earth to Maddie. Where are you going?"

I glance at Pip and notice she is motioning for us to follow her -- in the opposite direction from where I'm heading. Pip is leading us back to the Shell Ring, to the Wapaho, to report our -- my -- conversation with the dolphins.

"The wildfires must be heating the water somehow," I suggest to Sam.

"But you know that the wildfires have been miles away from the Sound, right? They couldn't heat it from so far away," Sam says gently.

"Sam, there must be a connection. We have to figure this out." Sam nods her agreement.

We emerge from the forest back into the Shell Ring and I spot Gilbius. He motions for us to follow him to his hut. Once we duck inside and settle ourselves onto our stumps, we tell him of our dolphin encounter.

"Gilbius, we need to find where the wildfires started. I think it might give us clues."

Gilbius shakes his head sadly, "I'm afraid there isn't much left to see, Maddie. The fires burned a clear path for miles before they could be extinguished."

But after one look at me, he engages in a short conversation with Pip. She quickly scoots out of the hut. Gilbius nods at me and tells us that Pipperdee is gathering a team to accompany us to the burn sites.

Outside, we find Pip and four other island guides waiting for us. They start walking briskly and we hurry to follow them underground.

Phew! We probably walk for miles in the spidery network of tunnels. My legs are so tired, but I know I have to keep going. For the dolphins. For the Wapaho. For the island.

Sam looks tired too, but she doesn't complain either.

Finally! Pipperdee leads us up a ladder and back into the forest. When we come up into the sunlight, we see the burned remains of trees and the scorched earth left from the fire's destruction.

The guides stop and look expectantly at me, as if waiting for directions. I chew on my lip while I'm deciding what to do. I don't know if I like being in charge.

Okay, let's see. First, we have to make sure that these were really wildfires. I read about a fire that destroyed a huge area in California. Police detectives discovered that the fire was started by a person, not by nature. That's called arson. Could that really be the case here? Would anyone actually want to hurt this island?

So to understand how the fire got started, we have to find where it first began. To do that, we'll have to split up and fan out around the edges of the burn path and trace it back to the starting point.

"Pip, why don't you come with me and Sam on one side and the rest of you take the other side?"

"Let's check the trees and look for the side that's black," I explain. "That will tell us what direction the fire was moving."

We run our fingers over the scorched trees and examine all the piles of ash scattered by the wind. We follow these clues until we meet the other guides coming from the other side.

"This must be the spot where the fire started! Let's all spread out and look around here for anything unusual."

We all begin searching for something. We don't even know what we're looking for. I hope I'm not leading us on a wild goose chase.

Wait! A clue!

"Hey!" I yell, hoping to get everyone to come take a look. In one scattered pile of ash I see what looks like a footprint, but I can't be sure. It looks stubby and thick, so it doesn't belong to a person. But, it still looks familiar. I know! It's a Wapaho footprint. Wait. What?

The guides look just as confused and concerned as I do. I can tell that they are thinking the same thing.

We keep searching near where we found the mysterious footprint. We don't find anything else, so we head back to the hatch to climb down into the tunnels for our return.

I feel pretty low as I walk behind Sam. We're all walking slower, disappointed that we haven't accomplished much on this journey. Just before I climb down the ladder, I turn with a sigh to look at the sad scene left by the fire. I survey the area one last time and... wait a sec! I see something.

Over in one of the largest piles of ash, not too far from the footprint, there's a tiny sparkle of orange shooting out. I ask Pip and the others to wait while

I dash over to check it out. As I approach the sparks, my dolphin locket starts to buzz and hum. I put a hand on it to steady it and absorb its energy.

I carefully poke a stick into the pile of ash to dig out the source of those sparks. I fish out what looks like a necklace with small charm in the shape of three flames. It looks like one of the emblems that the Wapaho wear around their necks.

I hold it up to examine it and see all of the guides standing nearby, looking slightly sick and staring with wide eyes.

"Bogsworth!" Pip gasps.

23

Betrayal

"**C**ome on, we've got to get back to see Gilbius!" Pip urges. She's running at full speed now. Even though she's probably only half our size, she's really fast, and Sam and I have to run as hard as we can to keep up.

Bogsworth. That's what Pipperdee said when she saw the charm I found. But what in the world is a Bogsworth?

Pip bursts through the door of Gillbius's hut. Sam and I follow closely behind. Gilbius, who was clearly taking a snooze in his chair, jerks awake. He seems a little dazed and confused at first, looking around the room and trying to make sense of what's going on.

As soon as Pipperdee hands him the charm with the flames, though, his eyes perk right up.

"Where did you find this?" he asks. His face goes pale, like he's just seen a ghost.

"Maddie found it at the burn site," replies Pip.

Gilbius looks at me like he's waiting for an explanation. "I looked at the burn patterns in the forest to figure out where one of the fires had started," I begin. "And when I found it, this was buried in the ashes. These fires weren't an accident. And, whoever started them was wearing this emblem."

"It can't be," Gilbius says. "How could he have become so powerful?"

"Who?" I ask.

"Bogsworth," Gilbius sighs, looking sad.

"Who is Bogsworth?"

"Bogsworth was one of us, a Wapaho. Until he was cast into exile many years ago."

"Why? What happened?" I question.

"The Forever Flamer changed him. You see, at one time, Bogsworth was a vital member of our tribe. His job was to make sure we always had fire, and he wore the emblem of the firemakers. Back then, he was kind, loyal and generous. Until he discovered the Forever Flamer.

"Created many years ago by the Native American elders and infused with their magic, the Forever Flamer gave its owner the power of flame, the power to bring fire whenever and wherever it was needed. Fire was just as important to the Native Americans as it is to us now, and the Forever

Flamer was their way of ensuring they always had it.

"Knowing how dangerous the Forever Flamer could be in the wrong hands, the elders always kept it hidden away, buried far beneath the ground. When they disappeared from this island so many years ago, no one knew what became of the Forever Flamer, and it faded into legend. Until..."

"Until Bogsworth found it!" I interrupt.

"Yes, Bogsworth found it. He thought its powers would bring good fortune to the tribe, which it did at first. But as the elders had feared so long ago, the Forever Flamer's powers proved too much for one person. Bogsworth became greedy with his new power. He began using the fire as a weapon, a way to get what he wanted from the others. And he came to believe that he, as owner of the Forever Flamer, was the rightful leader of the tribe. He demanded that he be recognized as King of the Wapaho.

"The tribe, however, did not want this. They, too, could see that he was no longer the kind-hearted Wapaho they once knew, and they rejected his claim to the tribal throne. Furious by this refusal, Bogsworth threatened to burn down our entire village if we did not recognize him as our King."

"And so what happened?" Sam asks.

"The tribe banded together and asked that he return the Forever Flamer to its original resting place underground. Rather than give up the Forever Flamer and its powers, he disappeared, and we haven't heard from him since. I knew he would remain a threat to us, but I never thought his powers could grow to this, not in the presence of the dolphin magic."

Dolphin magic?! In a flash, everything becomes clear to me.

"But that's just it!" I shouted excitedly. "The dolphins are leaving the island! That's why Bogsworth is getting stronger. And they're leaving because the water is getting too hot. If we could just figure out why the water is warming up, we could..."

"Maddie, what is it?! What were you going to say?" Sam asks.

"I've got it. I know why the dolphins are leaving! And I know how Bogsworth is doing it. Come on, we've got to get back to the tunnels!"

*
* *
*

24

Flame Thrower

As Sam and I race behind Pip, I rub my fingertip, remembering the heat from the holes I examined in the tunnels. It was all making sense now. Those hot, glowing holes must be heating the water. And I'd bet an ice cream sundae with sprinkles and a cherry that Bogsworth is behind it.

"Sam, I think Bogsworth is using his fire power to heat the water and drive the dolphins away. That's making him stronger and more dangerous to the island."

Sam opens her mouth to respond, but then we both spot a flash of orange and see the tunnel hatch slam closed. Pip sees it, too, and shoves us behind a sturdy oak tree with dangling moss.

We carefully peek around the edge of the tree, stretching to see the tunnel entrance. Sam and I gasp loudly to see a dingy, ash-covered Wapaho with glowing orange and red eyes sneering back at us. I'm sure I'll never forget those eyes with shifting sparkles like a blazing bonfire. Creeeeeepy.

"Bogsworth!" Pip whispers and waves us back behind the tree. But before we can get there, we notice a zig-zaggy, orange-and-white line zipping its way across the ground between us and the orange-eyed creeper. It is fizzing and popping like firecrackers.

"Whoa!" Sam and I can't take our eyes off the lines that are appearing on all sides of us, almost in a square, like it's boxing us in.

Pipperdee looks frightened and I soon see why. In a flash, those sparking lines burst into dancing flames so big that they jump taller than our heads. Bogsworth looks very pleased with himself.

Pipperdee, Sam and I all seem to realize at the same moment that this is not good. The box of flames is growing fast, burning through the pinestraw and mulch on the forest floor and closing in on us.

"Sam! The tree!" I point to a nearby tree and tug Sam along. "Climb!" I can barely choke out my words for the smoke.

But instead of climbing, she pushes me forward to the tree and runs towards the other side of the shrinking box of flames. I can only stand and watch, wondering what she is thinking.

"Go!" Pip says hoarsely to me and then follows Sam. Why am I the only one who can't figure out what's going on?

Wails and screams and a giant ruckus come from another tree, the one that Sam and Pipperdee are climbing. "Somebody help! We're trapped! It's getting hot! Ohhhhh!" I want to rush over to help them when Sam catches my eye and mouths, "Go!"

Oh! A distraction! I get it now. Bogsworth is all smiles, believing their award-winning performance. I refocus and scale the tree. I have to see if I can get to the tunnels and stop the fires that are heating the water. I think we're going to need those dolphins for sure.

I just have to figure out how to cross the blazing line of the fire box holding me captive. I'm on the highest branch that's strong enough to hold me. I inch out as far as I can go without it snapping off. If I can just get far enough out, I might be able to jump over the blaze.

I decide I'm just going to have to go for it. I have no other choice. I take a deep breath and try not to think about getting through the flames, how far down I'm going to fall and how hard the ground is. I close my eyes and fling my whole body forward, hoping I clear the fire box. I feel a flash of heat and then I crash down, my legs buckling under me.

Um, ouch.

But I'm okay! I'm scratched up and I'm sure my shin is going to have a humongous purple bruise, but I'm okay. Luckily, I landed in a massive pile of Spanish moss. It's pretty itchy, but sort of soft at the same time.

I look back through the blaze and I see Sam and Pipperdee still up in the tree, still hoarsely wailing and coughing. I can't be sure, but it sounds less and less like they are pretending now. I almost turn back to save them, but I know I have to get to those holes in the tunnels and see if I can stop the water warming.

I have to think. I can't see Bogsworth now, but the last time I saw him he was at the tunnel entrance. I know there are other entrances. But where?

I'm fiddling with the moss while I'm pondering my dilemma. I keep picking at a little pebble buried in the moss. When I finally glance down at what I'm fingering, I notice that it isn't a pebble at all. It's a seed -- a helicopter seed! That's it!

I've always loved helicopter seeds; at least that's what I call them. Mikey and I like to toss them up in the air and watch them spin and flutter down to the ground like little helicopters.

I remember seeing them by the tunnel entrances when we went to see the dolphins before and when we went to the burn site. Maybe that means the tunnel entrances are near maple trees. That's what makes the helicopter seeds. Last year I checked out a book on how to identify trees by their leaves and seeds. I meant to get a different book, but once I opened this one, I was hooked and I couldn't put it down. Now I can tell you about almost any tree I see.

Find a maple tree. Find a maple tree. I search around for the five-pointed leaves with red stems. No luck. No maple leaves anywhere. I can't give up, though. Maybe I need a new plan.

I stop for a moment, staring into space ahead of me, trying to figure out what to do. I catch sight of something fluttering out of the corner of my eye. A helicopter seed! I look behind me and see it! The maple tree. I scan the ground around the base of the tree and see nothing but dirt.

I kick the ground in frustration, scattering dirt and dust everywhere. When it settles, I notice I've uncovered the edge of what just might be... YES! It's a tunnel entrance!

25

Trapped

"You thought you could get the best of Bogsworth, did you?"

Bogsworth is circling the bottom of the tree that Sam and Pip are clinging to. There's no way for them to escape, and everyone knows it.

"You thought that two silly little girls and puny little Pipperdee could defeat the mighty Bogsworth, eh? Ha ha ha!" Bogsworth is laughing, but it's not a happy laugh. It's a seriously scary, I'm-about-to-do-something-really-terrible kind of laugh. Each time he speaks, he shoots another flame from his hand, lighting more and more of the forest on fire.

"Soon the waters of Hilton Head will be too hot for any of your dolphin friends, and my powers will grow beyond anything you could possibly imagine!" he sneers.

"Maddie was right," Sam whispers to Pip. "He is heating the waters. She has to hurry!"

"At last, I will be King of the Wapaho," Bogsworth continues, "Everyone will worship me, and all the Wapaho men, women and children will regret the day they cast off the powerful Bogsworth!"

With these last words, Bogsworth shoots two huge flames skyward. One of them catches the end of the branch that Sam and Pip are on and it begins to smoke. "Oh please, oh please, Maddie, get the dolphins back soon before we're turned to ash." Sam chants to herself.

26

Fire Extinguisher

"Okay, think Maddie, think!" I say to myself as I kneel down in front of all the little fire holes Bogsworth has drilled into the walls of the tunnel. I place my hand in front of one them. It's scorching! The flames must have strengthened inside since we were last here.

How do I put out a fire I can't even get to? That's not even possible!

Wait a sec. Heat, oxygen and fuel. Heat, oxygen and fuel. That's the fire triangle, the three things a fire needs to keep going. I remember it from the book on wildfires I'd gotten at the Hilton Head library.

Take one of those things away and the fire will die. But how on earth?

Wait a sec. The oxygen comes from the air, so the fire needs air to live. And the only way the air gets in is through these holes. That's it! Plug the holes so that no air gets in, and the fires will die!

I hit the ground and start grabbing huge clumps of sand with my hands, shoving them into the holes as fast as I can, trying to form a tight seal. This better work, or else Sam, Pip, and all the rest of Hilton Head Island are toast. Literally!

I just hope it's not too late for Sam and Pip. After I plug as many holes as I can, I sprint back through the tunnels towards the forest. Please be ok, please be ok.

27

Smoking Fingers

"Pip, this branch isn't gonna hold us much longer," Sam gasps. "The whole thing is almost on fire. We've gotta jump!" Pip nods. "On the count of three. One... two... three!"

Sam and Pip both hit the ground hard and then roll a few times, ending up right at the tip of Bogsworth's feet. "Oh, giving up, are we?" he says with a toothy sneer. "You're mine now!"

"Never!" Sam screams. She grabs Pip's hand and pulls her along as they scramble away. "Run, Pip, run!"

As Sam and Pip take off to flee from Bogsworth, Sam casts a quick glance back to see if he is following them. Sure enough, he's only a few feet away, and he's still cackling that crazed laugh.

With her eyes still fixed on Bogsworth, Sam doesn't spot the overgrown tree root sprouting from the ground in front of her. She trips, and she and Pip both crumble to the ground in a tangle. Bogsworth lets out another gleeful cackle, and is now standing right over them.

"I guess this is the end of the road for you two!" he howls.

He raises both hands over his head, his smoking fingers curled. "Say goodbye, little ones!"

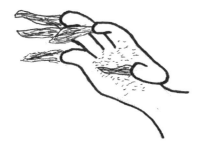

28

Powerless

As Bogsworth is about to light Sam and Pip into a ball of flames, I burst through the tunnel door.

"Sam! No!!!!!!!" I scream.

"Oh, I'm so glad you joined the farewell party. Especially since you're one of the three guests of honor!" Bogsworth hisses at me. "You can say goodbye to these two before it's your turn."

Bogsworth turns back to Sam and Pip and raises his arms to throw the flames that will engulf them. Just as he does, I do the only thing I can think of. I let out the loudest, most strangled and desperate scream I can muster.

But my scream doesn't help. Bogworth is still slinging his smoking fingers at my friends. Oh, I can't watch!

But wait, something is happening... Correction: nothing is happening! I peel my hands away from my eyes and see Sam and Pip doing the same. We are all gaping at Bogsworth, who is staring at his sparking fingers in bewilderment. They are making little sizzling sounds like a fire does when you pour water on it. But no flames. And no farewell to my friends! Wahoo!

Bogsworth catches us staring and his frown deepens. "Don't you worry, little ones, your time is coming. This is a job for my Forever Flamer."

His stubby fingers reach into a leather pouch tied at his waist and retrieve a metallic mushroomy thing. That must be the Forever Flamer I've heard so much about.

Now the sick feeling returns to my stomach. If this thing is as strong as Gilbius thinks it is, then we are all going to be toasted marshmallows -- again.

But as Bogworth holds up the Forever Flamer, a ray of sunlight streaming through the trees glints off the metal mushroom and the whole thing transforms into a pile of ash in his nubby hand. We watch as small bits of the dust slide through his fingers and float around in the sparkling ray of light.

"Noooooooooooooooooo!" he wails and he drops to his knees on the ground. His face is stricken with horror as he realizes that he has become powerless. "What did you do? How is this happening? It was all planned so perfectly..." he babbles to himself.

I rush to Sam and throw myself at her as we scoop each other into a big, squealing hug. And then we turn to Pip with questions in our eyes. "What now?" we wonder.

She points to my dolphin locket without a word. That's when Sam and I both notice that it's glowing again.

And then I remember. The dolphins! Plugging the holes must have worked!

29

A Change of Heart

"**O**h dear me, oh dear me. What have I done?" Bogsworth whimpers.

Bogsworth has finally realized that his powers are gone. He's sitting on the ground, curled up into a little ball and he's rocking back and forth.

"Please, please spare my life. Please let me live. I beg you."

"You tried to kill us!" Sam cries. "The only reason we're still alive is because the dolphins came back. Thanks to Maddie."

He doesn't look nearly so scary now. He seems weak and frail. In fact, he looks so pathetic that I almost feel sorry for him. I think he senses this, because he looks straight at me now. I notice that his eyes are now brown and green like the other Wapaho, instead of that creepy orange-ish color. He's about to say something until he catches a glimpse of the locket.

"Ah," he gasps. "You. Y-y-y-you're the wearer of the locket." Bogsworth then moves onto his knees and bows his head in front of me.

"Please, you must understand. You must help me. I didn't want all this to happen. It's just that the powers, being able to make fire, all of it was just too much. I found myself saying things, doing things that I didn't want to say or do. And before I knew it, everything I knew, everything I'd loved -- was gone. All because of what I'd done. I've done terrible things, I know that. Spare my life and let me go and I'll never bother anyone again."

I see Sam's face turn bright red. "No way! You can't get off that easily."

"How can we know you won't do something like this again?" Pip questions. "We can't let you loose after what you've done."

"They're right," I tell Bogsworth. "We can't just let you go and pretend this never happened. We're taking you back to camp. This is for Gilbius and the tribe to decide. When we get back, you stay quiet and let us explain what happened, okay?"

"Okay," Bogsworth whimpers. "I'm so very sorry."

*
* *
*
30

Forgiveness

am is angry and Pip seems both disappointed and sad. But I feel kind of bad for Bogsworth. Seeing him now, so pitiful and shaking with fear as we head back to face the tribe, I can't help but think how I would feel.

It reminds me of how I'm feeling about the not-so-nice things I said to my family.

Oh! My family! I bet my parents are so worried about where I am! Yikes, now I feel even worse.

As we enter the Shell Ring, it's a hive of commotion. Little Wapaho are rushing about everywhere, each wrapped up in their own job. It's life as usual, until we enter the ring. When we do, a hush falls over everyone as they discover who we have with us. By now they have all heard what Bogsworth was up to.

Suddenly, a group of Wapaho wearing mossy vests and bugle-emblem necklaces scoot off into all directions and start climbing trees. Upon reaching the first level of the branches in their trees, they begin to shake those branches and an amazing thing happens. Instead of hearing leaves rustling, I hear... bells. A little tinkling of bells begins to sound throughout the forest. The branches must have bells attached to them, too small to even see.

As the bells continue their soft melody, more Wapaho rush to encircle the Shell Ring. Wow. This is amazing. It's like an alarm, calling the tribe together. Not a loud, obnoxious sound like the alarm for our school fire drills, but a beautiful, peaceful alarm of bells.

I glance at Bogsworth, who keeps his eyes on the ground, not wanting to look at his old tribemates. Gilbius approaches with a serious look on his face. He opens his mouth to speak, but I stop him. I have to say this.

"Gilbius, before you decide what's to happen with Bogsworth, I need you to know that he understands what he's done. He's truly very sorry. He is. I can tell. We all make mistakes and need to make up for them. And I think he will. Make up for them, I mean. This is his home, his family. And that's what's important."

I look over my shoulder at Sam to see if she's angry with me for sticking up for Bogsworth since she is no fan of the fire flamer. I'm relieved to see her nodding at my words.

And for the first time, Bogsworth lifts his head reluctantly to look up at me and then at the tribe. His eyes are glossy with tears and he's nodding, too. Pip grabs his hand in hers.

Gilbius raises his arms and turns to the tribe with a question in his eyes. He's asking them to decide.

First one, and then a few more of the Wapaho place their hands on their hips and begin turning in circles. They each draw a circle around them in the dirt with a stubby toe. More and more of the Wapaho repeat the movement until they are all doing it.

I am fascinated watching this, wondering what it means. I look at Sam who is glued to the scene like she's watching TV. And that's when I hear Bogsworth wail and see tears streaming down his face.

Gilbius takes him in a big hug while we wonder what's happening. Then Gilbius releases him and turns to Sam and me to explain, "The tribe has accepted him. The circles they drew mean that they believe he has completed his wayward journey and has returned to his starting point of worthiness."

They have accepted him! I thought they would lock him up in a Wapaho jail forever.

"For a time, he will be under watch to make sure that he has no more slip-ups and that he is a good, contributing member of the tribe," Gilbius explains.

"But in time, I'm sure he will prove he is trustworthy and once again a friend to our beloved island."

"And we must thank you both, Maddie and Sam. Without you, Hilton Head Island may have been destroyed, along with our animal friends and our tribe."

Bogsworth's head again dips with Gilbius's words. He'll always carry this with him, what he's done. I'm just glad the tribe has shown forgiveness.

"Maddie, as wearer of the dolphin locket, you are a special friend to our people. And Sam, with your bravery to help save our people and our island, you, too, will always remain a friend of the Wapaho. We invite you to visit us whenever you return to the island."

He hands us each a small glass prism that reflects the sun's rays with a rainbow of colors. "Use these," he instructs. "They will help you locate the glitter lilies, the flowers that mark the entrance to The Hidden Forest."

I nod, remembering the sparkling plants that I wanted to photograph when I first made my way here.

Pip motions for us to follow her and I understand she's leading us out of their village. I wave to Bogsworth, Gilbius and the tribe, feeling kind of sad to leave them. But at least we can come back.

Sam and I hold hands as we follow Pip back to the garden of glitter.

31

Family Reunion

"Look at that flower, Maddie!" Sam exclaims, pointing towards a glittering orange blossom. It looks like it's studded with tiny little silver polka dots, but every so often the little polka dots launch into the air like fireworks and then disappear into a shower of green sparks.

"Whoa, that's amazing!" I say. "I'm so gonna miss this place."

"Me, too."

I'm starting to recognize the path we're on and all the flowers around me. This is the path I took when I first entered The Hidden Forest. We must be nearing the portal back to the Forest Preserve.

"And we're gonna miss you too, Pip!"

Pip stops walking for a second and looks back at me. She nods her head slowly up and down and lets out a sad little squeak.

"But we have the prisms, so we can come back and see you guys during our next vacation."

Pip starts nodding a lot faster and gives us a big smile. She takes a few more steps forward and then stops. She extends her arm straight out in front of her as if she's showing us something.

In front of us where Pip is gesturing, I see a tree with branches split into a wide V-shape. And on the base of the tree, very small, is a golden emblem that's been engraved with the seal of the Wapaho.

"This is the portal entrance, isn't it, Pip?"

She nods. Then she holds both arms wide open, asking for a hug.

I grab her under her arms and lift her into the air. She squeals and starts kicking her legs gleefully.

"I need a hug, too!" Sam says. She puts her arms around the both of us, and we have one big group hug.

"Thanks for everything you've done for us, Pip" I say.

"It is you two who should be thanked, Maddie and Sam. Thanked for saving me. Thanked for saving my tribe. Thanked for saving Hilton Head Island."

I smile at Pip then lower her back to the ground. "Ready, Sam?"

"Ready."

We grasp hands then walk through the portal.

After just a few steps, it's clear things are different again. No more glowing flowers shooting fireworks. I look behind me at the portal. No more Pip.

"I know where we are." Sam says.

"Yep, me too. The main path for the Forest Preserve is just up ahead," I reply. I know the way out.

"How long have we been gone, Maddie?" Sam asks.

"I really have no idea. A week, maybe? Maybe several weeks?"

"Our parents are probably so worried. I'm sure the police are looking for us."

"Our pictures are probably on the news."

"And how in the world are we going to explain to them where we've been? If we tell them truth, they'll never believe us!"

"I know." As my mind starts to swirl, concocting possible stories about what happened to us, I'm interrupted by a little trill of music playing right next to my foot. Wait a sec -- could that be another magical flower? Are we still in the The Hidden Forest?

Then I realize something: I know that sound!

"Sam, that's my Mom's ringtone!" I shout. I look down and, sure enough, there's my mom's cell phone case with a picture of me and Mikey on it.

"Answer it!" Sam shouts.

"Hello?" I say.

"Maddie, is that you? I take it you found mom's phone!"

"Yes, it's me dad, it's me!" I'm jumping up and down now. I've never been so happy to hear my dad's voice.

"Well, we were about to walk out of the Forest Preserve when we noticed you still hadn't come back to join us after you stormed off. So we started walking back into the forest to try to find you. Then mom noticed her cell phone had fallen out of her pocket somewhere, so we decided to give it a call."

"Wait a sec, dad. You mean you're still here? In the Forest Preserve?"

"Sure we are, Maddie."

"You've been waiting this whole time?!"

"Whole time? Maddie, are you feeling alright? It's only been about five minutes since you left us."

Whoa. Five minutes?! It's like going to The Hidden Forest never even happened.

"By the way, is Sam with you?"

"Yes. How'd you know?"

"We ran into her parents. They were looking for her, too. We figured you two might be together."

"Okay, dad. We'll be right there." I end the call.

"My parents and your parents are both at the Lawton entrance. Let's go!"

We both start running. Sprinting, actually. As fast as we can.

"Mom! Dad! Mikey!" I shout once they come into view.

"Mom! Dad!" Sam yells.

We get to the entrance and we're both totally out of breath.

"Mom and dad, I'm so sorry for the way I acted earlier, and for what I said. I didn't mean any of it. I'll make it up to you, I promise."

"It's okay, Maddie. We know you were just frustrated. Sometimes little brothers have their special way of getting on your nerves," my mom says with a grin.

"Well, you're not on my nerves anymore, Mikey. You're the best little brother I could have."

"Hey mom, get your camera out. Let's try that picture of Mikey and me again."

As I'm saying this, I give Mikey a huge hug. I'm so happy to see him, too. He looks totally confused.

"Uh, ok," he says. Mom snaps her picture.

"Well that one's a keeper for sure!" my mom says. "Thank you, Maddie.

As I'm hugging Mikey, I notice he's now got his head cocked to the side and is looking sideways at my neck.

"Hey!" he exclaims "Where'd you get that locket?!"

Same old Mikey. He's back to being my annoying little brother. I bug my eyes out at him to let him know that I want him to STOP TALKING. The last thing I need is to have questions about this locket that I can't explain.

Thankfully, Mikey gets the hint, although he still sticks his tongue out at me. I quickly, but carefully, remove the locket and slip it into my pocket. My pocket has a zipper on it, so I can close it up and the locket will be safe.

When Mikey first started yelling about the locket, my dad turned to see what was going on. I thought he was on to me, but then he got distracted talking to Sam's dad about going to the beach. Phew. That was close.

*

32

A Freckled Friend

Mikey is sitting down the beach from us, building a sand racetrack for his trucks and cars. Our parents are busy lounging and laughing like they've known each other forever, while Sam and I sit on our towels and relive our adventure. It's like we need to talk about it to believe that it really happened.

We both notice that all the beach walkers are stopping to stare at the water. I wonder if there's a shark.

We begin to notice fins popping up out of the water everywhere. But those aren't sharks, the fins are too curved.

"Maddie, look!" Sam yells. "There! And there! And... so many, Maddie!"

We grab hands and rush down to the water, spraying sand along our hurried path. I stop just as my toes meet the cool waves and I take it all in. Sam and I watch as the dolphins gather in front of me. It's beautiful.

"They're waiting for you, Maddie," Sam urges me forward.

I walk deeper into the water until it reaches my chest and feel the dolphins swish past me on all sides. They splash, puff air from their blowholes and giggle with their high-pitched squeals.

"They're happy, Sam." She nods, laughing.

Then I spy a familiar freckled fin poking through the water.

"Hey, I know you," I tell him softly.

"You remember when we met?" he squeaks.

"Oh yes. You seem much happier now." I'm smiling so big my cheeks hurt.

"That's because of you, Maddie. You saved us. The island's dolphins, the forest animals, the Wapaho and even the island itself. You saved everything."

I look down at my hands and then shyly reach out to gently pat his side. I shake my head, "Not really. I didn't do anything special. Anyone could just have easily done the same if they'd had the locket."

"Not just anyone, Maddie. The locket revealed itself to you because you are like us in so many ways, just like Gilbius said. You were meant to find it, Maddie, because the island needed you."

I continue to pet his side while I try to absorb his words. I feel tears welling up in my eyes. "I hope I'll see you again. I'll come see you every time I come to Hilton Head. And I'll bring my locket!" He bobs his head up and down like he's nodding.

I don't want this moment to end, but I soon hear splashing and a great commotion as Mikey screams, "Dolphin! Dolphin! I want to touch one!"

The dolphin pod circles me and Sam and then heads farther out into deeper waters.

Oh, Mikey.

33

The Most Magical Place

"Come on, Maddie. Time to go!" my dad beckons from the car.

"Be right there."

Our car is all packed up and ready to go. I'm stealing a last glance at the water before getting in, trying to see if I can spot one final glimpse of a dolphin fin poking through the water. No matter how many times I see them, they never get old.

Everyone on the island is talking about how they can't remember the last time there were so many dolphins playing in the water.

I climb in the back seat next to Mikey. "Ready, guys?" dad asks.

"Ready." Mikey and I reply.

As our car heads out of the parking lot onto South Sea Pines Drive, Mikey and I turn to each other and smile. We know what to do next.

"Is that a booger in the sugar? No, it's not," we start singing together.

"Is that a booger in the sugar? No, it's not!"

Dad looks back at me and Mikey through the rear view mirror and makes a pretend mean face, then shakes his fist in the air. "Don't you guys start with me," he says.

"Dad, we made a promise to Gregg Russell," Mikey replies.

"That rotten Gregg Russell. I'm gonna have to write him a nasty letter!" dad says jokingly.

Then dad smiles real big and starts singing, "though I had a bunch for lunch, you can hear the suckers crunch! Is that a booger in the sugar? No, it's not!"

As Mikey and my parents keep singing, I look out the window. We're about to pass the Forest Preserve, and I want to see it one last time before we leave.

My phone buzzes in my pocket. It's a text message from Sam:

>> hey maddie mack. i've got good news! <<

>> hey sam! <3 what's that??? <<

>> my mom talked to ur mom about next summer, and we're gonna be here the same week again! <<

>> that's so awesome!!!!! <<

>> i know :-) and don't forget to bring it next year. <<

>> bring what??? <<

>> this. <<

Sam texts me a picture. It's the prism.

>> of course. i can't wait to go back and see everyone!! <<

>> talk to u soon. hugs! <<

>> hugs! bye, sam. <<

I reach into my pocket and rub the locket between my fingertips. Sometimes I find myself wondering if all of this really happened. I wonder if all of it was just a dream. The locket helps me remember that it wasn't.

And I think about what my dolphin friend said, that I was chosen to wear the locket. Am I really all those things Gilbius said? Courageous, loyal, curious and kind, just like the dolphins? It's a lot to live up to, but I'm gonna try my hardest to prove them right.

We're passing the Forest Preserve now. I look out at all the live oak trees with the wispy Spanish moss hanging down, blowing gently in the breeze. It's so peaceful it almost lulls me to sleep.

But then I see something in one of the trees. It looks like... a face!

It's Pip! She's peeking out from one of the trees and waving. How in the world did she know?!

As I'm waving back I notice that Pip looks like she's floating in the air. Wait a sec -- she's not floating, she's sitting on somebody's shoulders. Bogsworth's shoulders!

Bogsworth is beaming from ear to ear, and he's waving, too. And I see that he now has the firemaker emblem around his neck. They really have accepted him.

I wave back to Bogsworth and our eyes meet. When they do, he mouths the words "thank you" to me. "You're welcome," I mouth back in return.

We pass through the Sea Pines exit, and the forest retreats into the distance. I didn't think it was even possible, but this was the best Hilton Head vacation I've had yet. And to think, without my help, this place would've been gone for good.

Locket or no locket, I'll always do anything it takes to protect this island. It's the most magical place in the world.

Become a
Vacation Adventure Girl

Be the first to know where the next vacation adventure takes place by heading over to vacationadventuregirl.com/club. There you can also sign up and become a member of the Vacation Adventure Girls Club. As a club member, you'll receive the very latest Vacation Adventure Girl news, get special bonuses just for members, and receive an early copy of the next book in the series.

Want your own dolphin locket like the one Maddie wore? Visit
vacationadventuregirl.com/dolphinlocket to get yours!

Want to stay in the same villa in Hilton Head where Maddie stays? Reserve your own vacation there by going to maddiesvilla.com. You might just find a special surprise or two waiting for you there!

Made in the USA
Lexington, KY
03 December 2018